Written by Dave Cudd

Illustrations by Brendan Mauer

From time to time
I let out a burp.
My Mother says it's fine,
As long as I excuse me,
It's nothing but a burp.

PIZZA
GRAPES
BREAD
EGGS
FLOUR
CINNAMON
BURP

But every now and then that burp

Comes from my bottom.

My Dad laughs out loud,

My Mom says, “Phew!”

And I make sure to say, “Excuse me.”

BURP
Excuse me.

I've been told that it's natural.
And I know firsthand I'm not alone.
Everyone has let out a sound
From down below.

When my Dad burps in the shower,
It sounds just like a boat.
And for full effect he exclaims,
"This boat is pulling out!"

BURP

Mom waits till no one is around
To let out a squeaky burp.
She blames the cat,
But who believes that.

COOKIE
BURP
BURP
BURP

My sister smiles real big,
When she lets out a burp.
She must think she's funny,
Or it must tickle her tummy.

BURP

I’ve never heard the dog burp
But I know when it’s been done,
I make sure to hold my breath
Then turn and run!

BURP

Granny’s are quite random
And if you ask her, she’ll deny.
Saying she didn’t hear that noise,
That came from her behind.

BURP
BURP

Grandpa always asks
If I can find the frog who's croaking?
Then lets one rip,
I think he's only joking.

BURP

My Uncles bet on who's the loudest.

I take their bet,

Then we count to three,

Before we let one free.

BURP
BURP
BURP

So when it's time
To let one burp,
I know I'm fine.
As long as I excuse me.

Excuse me!
BURP

Parents,

Thanks for reading to your children. With each word your child's world expands, and their appreciation for reading grows. As you read this book have your child excuse each member of the family for their flatulence.

For free coloring sheets and to find out more about my projects head over to www.DaveCudd.com

Thank you for supporting our work.

This book uses OpenDyslexic typeface which can be downloaded for free at http://opendyslexic.org

Made in the USA
Columbia, SC
06 February 2019